Sports World

Track and Field

Donna Bailey

Steck-Vaughn
COMPANY
ELEMENTARY · SECONDARY · ADULT · LIBRARY

Running, jumping, and throwing are all part of track and field. Running may look easy, but like all other sports, it requires skill and practice.

Runners wear shorts and a T-shirt
during an event.
Sometimes they have special shoes
with spikes to grip the ground.
A track suit keeps them warm afterward.

The runners take their places at the beginning of a sprint race. When they hear "On your mark," they crouch down behind the starting line.

On the order "Get set," the athletes
lift up their bodies to get a good start.
"Go" or a pistol shot is the signal
to start running.
The runners start off as fast as they can.

Some athletes use a starting block at the beginning of a race to help them get away faster.

Sprint races are run over distances
of 100, 200, and 400 meters.
The athletes run as fast as they can
to reach the finish line.

Middle distance races cover
from 800 meters to 1,500 meters.
Athletes run these longer races at
a slower pace.
At the end of the race, they give
a final burst of speed.

Long distance races are run
from 3,000 meters to 30,000 meters.
The athletes run at a steady pace
during the whole race.
To win these races, it is more important
to keep running than to run fast.

A marathon is a long distance race
which is run mainly on roads or paths.
Thousands of runners take part in
the New York and Boston marathons.

These athletes are running in
a cross-country race.
They run through woods and open fields.
Often they must cross creeks and ravines.

Relays are run by teams of runners.
These races have four stages called legs.
The runner finishing one leg must
pass a baton to the next runner.

The next runner holds out his hand
behind him as he starts to run.
The first runner passes the baton.
Each runner is careful not to drop it.

Hurdlers run races over a series of gates called hurdles.
The athletes sprint between the gates and use their arms to help them jump over the hurdles.

A hurdler tries not to break her stride
when she jumps a hurdle.
She lifts her back leg over the hurdle
in such a way that she keeps on running.

A steeplechase race is run
on an obstacle course.
The obstacles on the course are ditches,
water jumps, and fences.

Races are usually run in lanes around the outside of a track.
Field events are the jumping and throwing events that take place in the center of the track.

Both men and women take part in field events.
This man is throwing a javelin.
He pulls back his throwing arm
as he runs up to the line.

18

He throws the javelin over his shoulder
on the last stride.
He uses his whole body to put as
much power into the throw as possible.

A discus looks like a flying saucer.
Before a throw, the athlete grips
the discus and spins around rapidly.

He lets go of the discus when his body is spinning at its fastest.

A shot is a smooth, heavy, round ball.
Before a throw, the athlete holds the shot
against his neck and faces backward.
Then he whirls around to push the shot off.
He uses the muscles in his legs and body
to make the shot go as far as possible.

Athletes use both hands to throw the hammer.
They spin around three or four times
and then let go of the hammer.

High jumpers need a well-padded area to land on after a jump.

To do a Fosbury flop, the high jumper takes a run up to the cross bar. As she runs, she turns her upper body. She pushes off from one foot and jumps backward over the bar.

The jumper arches her back and bends her knees to keep from touching the cross bar. Then she falls to the landing pad.

26

In a pole vault, the athlete also jumps
over a bar without knocking it off.
Pole vaulters use long poles which bend.
The athlete runs toward the bar and plants
the pole in a box in front of the bar.

As the pole straightens, the athlete rides the pole and rises up into the air.

Then he lets go of the pole and twists his body to get over the bar.

Long jumpers run at full speed down
the track before they jump.

30

A long jumper uses her arms and legs
to help throw her body forward.
She lands heels first in the sand pit.

In the triple jump, the athlete first hops
and lands on his take-off foot.
Then he takes a step to land on
the other foot before jumping as
far as he can to land in the sandpit.

Index

baton 12, 13
clothes 3
cross-country races 11
discus throw 20, 21
finish line 7
Fosbury flop 25
hammer throw 23
high jump 24, 25, 26
hurdles 14, 15
javelin throw 18, 19
jumping 2, 17, 24, 25, 26, 27, 28, 29, 30, 31, 32
long distance races 9
long jump 30, 31
marathons 10, 11
middle distance races 8
pole vault 27, 28, 29

relay races 12, 13
running 2, 4, 5, 6, 7, 8, 9, 10, 11, 12, 13, 14, 15, 16, 17
shoes 3
shot put 22
sprint race 4, 7
starting 4, 5
starting block 6
starting line 4
steeplechase races 16
throwing 2, 17, 18, 19, 20, 21, 22, 23
track 17
triple jump 32

Editorial Consultant: Donna Bailey
Executive Editor: Elizabeth Strauss
Project Editor: Becky Ward

Picture research by Jennifer Garratt
Designed by Richard Garratt Design

Photographs
All photographs by Peter Greenland except:
Cover: Sporting Pictures
All Sport: 23 (Diane Johnson)
Robert Harding: 16
Sporting Pictures: 9, 10, 11, 17

Library of Congress Cataloging-in-Publication Data: Bailey, Donna.   Track and field / Donna Bailey. p.   cm.— (Sports world) Includes index. Summary: Describes the skills and techniques used in the running, jumping, throwing, and vaulting events that make up track and field sports. ISBN 0-8114-2901-6 1. Track-athletics—Juvenile literature.   [1. Track and field.] I. Title.   II. Series: Bailey, Donna. Sports world. GV1060.5.B26 1991 796.42—dc20 90-23053 CIP AC

Trade Edition published 1992 © Steck-Vaughn Company

ISBN 0-8114-2901-6 hardcover library binding   ISBN 0-8114-4747-2 softcover binding
Copyright 1991 Steck-Vaughn Company
Original copyright Heinemann Children's Reference 1991
All rights reserved. No part of the material protected by this copyright may be reproduced or utilized in any form or by any means, electronic or mechanical, including photocopying, recording, or by any information storage and retrieval system, without permission in writing from the copyright owner. Requests for permission to make copies of any part of the work should be mailed to: Copyright Permissions, Steck-Vaughn Company, P.O. Box 26015, Austin, Texas 78755. Printed in the United States of America.

2 3 4 5 6 7 8 9 0 LB 96 95